*For my son, Tim, who is deciding
what to do with the rest of his life*

Requests for permission to make copies of any part of the work should be
mailed to: Permissions Department, Harcourt Brace & Company,
6277 Sea Harbor Drive, Orlando, Florida 32887-6777.

First published in Great Britain in 1998 by Andersen Press Ltd.
First U.S. edition 1999

Library of Congress Cataloging-in-Publication Data
McNaughton, Colin.
Yum!/Colin McNaughton.
p.   cm.
Summary: Preston Pig suggests that Mr. Wolf get a job so he can buy what he wants
to eat, but as he considers different lines of work, Mr. Wolf has a one-track mind.
ISBN 0-15-202064-0
[1. Pigs—Fiction.   2. Wolves—Fiction.]   I. Title.
PZ7.M4787935Yu   1999
[E]—dc21   98-27980

A C E F D B

Printed and bound in Italy by Grafiche AZ, Verona

No animals were hurt in the
making of this book. Oh, except
Mr. Wolf, of course.

Colin McNaughton

Yum!

Harcourt Brace & Company
San Diego   New York   London

"So, clever chops," said Mr. Wolf, "what kind of job do you suggest?"
"What do you want to be?" said Preston.
"Well. . .," said Mr. Wolf.
"Full."
"What are you good at?" said Preston.

"Well...," said Mr. Wolf.
"Eating pigs."
"And what do you enjoy?"
said Preston.
"Well...," said Mr. Wolf.
"Eating pigs *and* being full."

"You could be a soccer player," said Preston. "Yum!" said Mr. Wolf. "I wouldn't mind a shot at that."

"You could be a
schoolteacher,"
said Preston.
"Yum!" said Mr. Wolf.
"Little pigs are so sweet!"

"You could be a
pilot," said Preston.
"Yum!" said Mr. Wolf.
"I do like an in-flight snack."

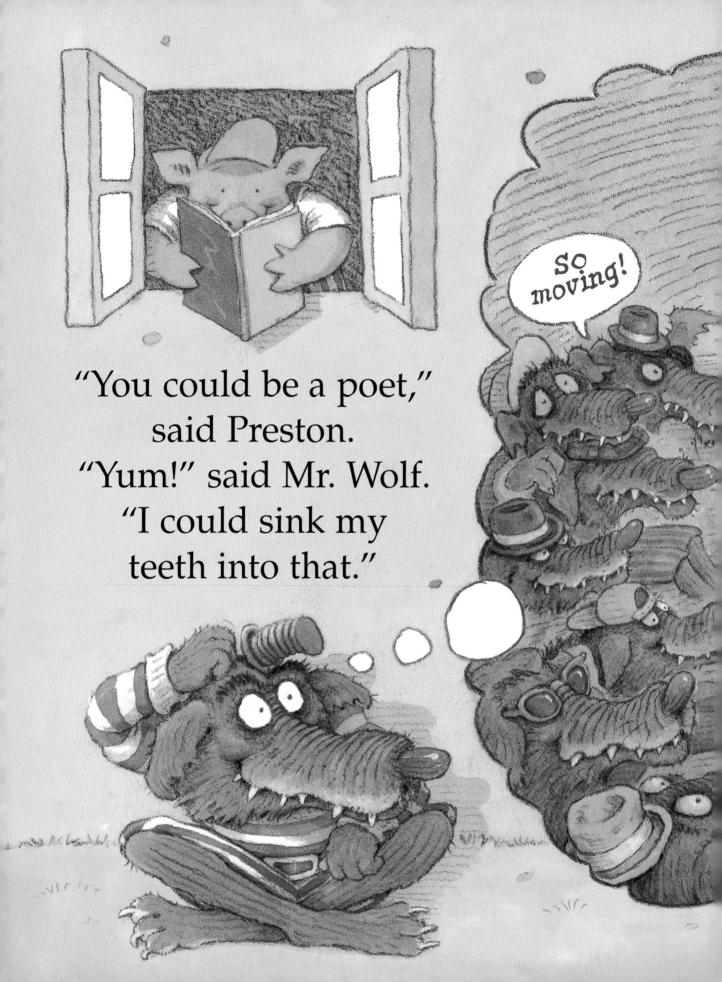

"You could be a poet,"
said Preston.
"Yum!" said Mr. Wolf.
"I could sink my
teeth into that."

So moving!

"You could be a crane driver," said Preston. "Yum!" said Mr. Wolf. "You've hit on a delicious idea!"

"You could be a sailor," said Preston. "Yum!" said Mr. Wolf. "That's a tasty thought."

"You could be a cook,"
said Preston.
"Yum!" said Mr. Wolf.
"I've got the perfect recipe!"

"So, Mr. Wolf,"
said Preston,
"what do you think?"

"Yum!" said Mr. Wolf.
"It's certainly
food for thought!"

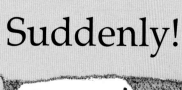
Suddenly!